FRANKLY FRANNIE

Funny Business

by AJ Stern

illustrated by Doreen Mulryan Marts

Grosset & Dunlap
An Imprint of Penguin Group (USA) Inc.

For Lili Stern, my muse.—AJS

Thanks as always to everyone at Penguin: Francesco
Sedita, Bonnie Bader, Caroline Sun, Scottie Bowditch, and
Jordan Hamessley. Also to Doreen Mulryan Marts, who
draws Frannie just like I'd pictured her, and my editor, Judy
Goldschmidt. Your support and enthusiasm is unparalleled!
To Julie Barer, of course, and her assistant, William
Boggess. To my family and friends for their support. And
of course to my nieces and nephew: Maisie, Mia, Lili, and
Adam, without whom I'd have lost touch long ago with the
bane and beauty of kid linguistics.—AJS

GROSSET & DUNLAP
Published by the Penguin Group
Penguin Group (USA) Inc., 375 Hudson Street, New York, New York 10014, USA
Penguin Group (Canada), 90 Eglinton Avenue East, Suite 700, Toronto,
Ontario M4P 2Y3, Canada (a division of Pearson Penguin Canada Inc.)
Penguin Books Ltd., 80 Strand, London WC2R 0RL, England
Penguin Group Ireland, 25 St. Stephen's Green, Dublin 2, Ireland
(a division of Penguin Books Ltd.)
Penguin Group (Australia), 250 Camberwell Road, Camberwell, Victoria 3124,
Australia (a division of Pearson Australia Group Pty. Ltd.)
Penguin Books India Pvt. Ltd., 11 Community Centre,
Panchsheel Park, New Delhi—110 017, India
Penguin Group (NZ), 67 Apollo Drive, Rosedale, North Shore 0632, New Zealand
(a division of Pearson New Zealand Ltd.)
Penguin Books (South Africa) (Pty.) Ltd., 24 Sturdee Avenue,
Rosebank, Johannesburg 2196, South Africa

Penguin Books Ltd., Registered Offices: 80 Strand, London WC2R 0RL, England

Library of Congress Control Number: 2010034451

ISBN 978-0-448-45540-2 (pbk)   10 9 8 7 6 5 4 3 2 1
ISBN 978-0-448-45541-9 (hc)   10 9 8 7 6 5 4 3 2 1

CHAPTER

"This is exciting, isn't it?" my mom asked, squeezing my hand. It certainly was very exciting. We were standing in line to board an **actual** airplane—for the first time ever in my worldwide life.

"Yes!" I said. "Very exciting, indeed." *Indeed* is a grown-up word I try to use as oftenly as possible.

"Maybe you'll get to meet the pilot!" my dad said as the line started to move.

That is when **my face almost**

fell off the earth. "A person can do that?" I asked.

"I don't see why not," he answered as we walked down the long and skinny-ish hallway that led to the airplane. My breath was so excitified because we were going to Florida where it's summer all the time!

When we stepped onto the plane, I saw three very important people. I knew they were important because they were wearing **uniforms**. It is a scientific fact that uniforms are very workerish.

Just then, the pilot stepped out of his office. I liked him right away because when he saw me, a smile grew on his face. I also liked him because he had an office. If you don't already know this about me, **I love offices**.

"Welcome aboard!" he said to me.

"Thank you," I answered.
"Welcome aboard to you, too!"

The other uniform people were busy helping other passengers, but I could tell they heard me because they laughed. That's when my dad introduced me to them.

"This is Frannie B. Miller—"

But before he could finish, there was something I needed to **remind** him about.

"It's actually Frankly," I said. "Mrs. Frankly B. Miller, to be exact," I handed the pilot one of my homemade business cards. He looked at it with a very big, **pilot smile**.

Frankly is a really grown-up word my parents use. It also sounds a lot like my actual name, Frannie, so I use it when I need to sound official. Except for sometimes when I forget.

I must have sounded **really official** this time because right after I told

him my name was Frankly, the pilot asked me if I wanted to see the **cockpit!**

There were so many buttons and levers in the cockpit, I didn't know how in the worldwide of America the pilot remembered which one did what. He must have been a real **genius**. I loved all the levers, but I also loved the **gold butterfly pin** he was wearing. I could not stop staring at it. That's when he caught me, which was very humilifying, indeed and nevertheless. But, you will not even believe your ears about what happened next.

The pilot took out the same gold butterfly pin from his pocket and gave it to me. When I looked at it, I saw it wasn't a butterfly.

"They're wings," he told me.

I WOWED him with my eyeballs.

"They're for top-level people," he

said. "Only pilots wear them. And Franklys," he said, with a very professional look in his eyes.

"I'm a top-level person?" I asked him.

"You are, indeed."

I could not in my worldwide life believe I was a **top-level** person. Top-level sounded very important.

After I left the cockpit, my mom, dad, and I walked to our seats. My dad put our bags into cubbies above our heads. When I sat down, I buckled myself in and looked around. Our seats were in Business Class, which is where you sit if you're going on a **business trip**.

A business trip is when your father has to go to Florida for his job. While we were going to be in

Florida, we were also going on a trip to Princessland, but there aren't any special airplane seats for that.

Some people were already doing their business, so I opened my briefcase, which used to be my dad's, and pulled out my own work. My work was an **activity pack** with drawing paper, a book of mazes and riddles and magic tricks, and three reading books. It also had cardboard so I could make more **business cards** if I needed to.

The airplane ran really fast when it was taking off and then it rose like a balloon into the sky. When we got up really high, I could see the clouds up close! This was a very special thing to see.

I would love to have a job with an **office in the clouds**! I was certainly going to give the pilot my résumé when we got off the plane. A résumé is a list of jobs you've had, and I've already had a **machillion**. That's why I am a top-level person.

CHAPTER

On the way to the Florida hotel, our driver told us to look outside the window past the highway. A little bit of **Princessland** was peeking out from behind the trees. We could see Ferris wheels, roller coasters, and the tops of three **castles**. I could not wait, wait, wait to go.

After three centuries and a decade of miles, we made it to the hotel. I don't know enough words to describe how **gigantoristic** it was.

There was a fountain right in the center of the lobby with water shooting out of a really short chimney. There were a millionteen desks all over the place. Each one had a sign telling us what it was all about. When I got home I had to remember to make signs that said "**Check-In**" and "**Information**" and turn my bedroom into a hotel.

There were lots of people wearing black T-shirts with HH on them. They all wore headphones and sometimes

one of them would talk into a walkie-talkie! Each person I saw seemed more professional than the last one. I could barely keep my breath together just thinking about all the exciting people I would meet.

"Hey, nice wings!" said the check-in lady with a name tag that said RUBY. That's when I remembered that I was still wearing the wing pin the pilot gave me. I gave Ruby the biggest top-level smile of ever.

Ruby checked us in and told us that if we needed anything else we should just ask the **Hotel Helpers**. Then, she pointed to the people with the HH's on their shirts. That's when I figured out that HH stood for Hotel Helpers!

"Your room number is five seventeen. If you want to order lunch by the **pool**, just tell the waiter your room number and he'll put it on your bill," Ruby told us.

Lunch by the pool sounded exactly like something I wanted to eat. *517. 517. 517. 517.*

It is a scientific fact that if you repeat something in your head, you will never forget it, ever.

Even though this was the only place in America I'd ever traveled to, it was so far my favorite.

517.

CHAPTER

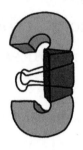

Our hotel room opened up by slipping a card into a slot above the doorknob. When the light turned green, it meant **we won** and could go inside. Red meant we had to play again.

The hotel room was like an actual apartment! There were two bedrooms, one living room, and a kitchen. The professional name for this type of hotel room is *suite.*

"Frannie, look!" my mom called as

she slid open the balcony door. I thought the balcony was going to be the *Frannie, look!* thing she wanted to show me. But, when my feet stepped outside, my eyes saw the balcony was only the second most special thing. When I looked down, I gasped my entire head off. Right below us was a swimming pool **the size of Chester**. There were a machillion people swimming in it and there were THREE diving boards. One low one, one middle one, and one really high one that I would never, in **twenty-eighteen** years, go on.

"How about we unpack, put on our bathing suits, and then go down to the pool?" my dad called from the other room.

"Sounds like heaven to me," my mom said, and we closed the balcony door behind us.

I went into the second room of the

suite, which actually was **all mine!**
I looked at every centimeter of my
room and opened every drawer that
ever existed. Inside one, I found a very
official-looking binder with lots of
hotelish things inside. A for instance
of what I mean is there was a room
service menu and a lot of chapters
about the entire hotel!

I ran into my parents' room to show
them.

"Look! A hotel book!"

"You can bring that to the pool
with you," my dad said.

"Really?"

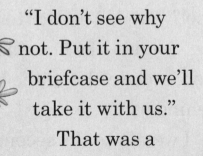

"I don't see why
not. Put it in your
briefcase and we'll
take it with us."

That was a

geniusal idea. I ran back to my room, put on my bathing suit, opened my briefcase, and very carefully put the thick, black binder inside. Then, I click-clicked the briefcase shut and followed my parents down the long hall to the elevator and toward the **biggest pool in America**.

CHAPTER

When we got to the pool, I wanted to read the hotel book, but I also wanted to swim. That is when I got a geniusal idea. I jumped in the pool and swam around for **three million** seconds. Then I climbed out, sat on my chair, and read the hotel book. After a page, I went back to the pool and did the **same thing**. I was going to do this until the book ran out of pages.

A waiter came over to our area and

my parents ordered two hamburgers and a **hot dog** because that's my favorite. When the waiter returned with our food, he said, "Can I have your room number, please?"

My mother turned to look at me. She probably heard my brain question: *Please, can I tell him our room number?????* She nodded at me, answering *yes* to my brain question.

"Five seventeen," I said very proudly.

My parents were proud right back. Then they clinked their glasses together and said, "To the Millers!" which is a for instance of what we say when we clink glasses or before we eat dinner. Then my dad turned to me with an **announcement face**.

"So, listen, Bird," my dad began. Bird is my middle name, but please do not tell **anyone** that. "Tonight, Fred Tilson, a co-worker of mine, is going to meet us for dinner."

"Because he is on the business trip, too?" I asked.

"That's right," my dad said. "And he brought his little girl also. Her name is Henrietta."

I scrunched my face up at her **weird** name.

"So we're having dinner with both of them."

"With the mom, too?" I asked.

"No, Henrietta's mom isn't here. She had to stay home because of her job."

"Oh," I said, very interested. "What's her job?"

"I think she's a dentist. You can ask Henrietta."

A dentist! That was the one kind of office I do not like visiting. "That's okay, I'm not so interested in jobs about teeth," I told him. "How old is Henrietta, anyway?" I asked.

"I think she's around eleven."

Eleven! Eleven made my face unscrunch. I love eleven-year-olds because they're older than me, and I love people who are older than me.

"They're from California," my dad told me.

California! That was the other place where it was summer all the time! I had a feeling that Henrietta was going to be a really **fancy** type of person.

"And, she's going to come to Princessland with us tomorrow, Frannie. Isn't that exciting?" my mom asked. I nodded.

I could not wait to meet Henrietta! And that is when my mind started to daydream about being at the **amusement park** with her. My parents were still talking, but not really about anything my ears thought was important. A for instance of what I mean is that my mother asked, "What time are they meeting us for dinner?" And my dad answered, "Six thirty."

See what I mean about **not important**?

I got back into the swimming pool, and when I came out, my mom put more sunblock on me. When she rubbed it on my back, I got to watch all the hotel workers do their jobs. I did not know whether I should be a pilot or a hotel worker. Pilots have a real office and hotel workers do not. However and nevertheless, I did not think I could memorize all the **pilot buttons** but I thought I could remember room numbers. *517.*

"Are you listening, Birdy?" my dad said.

"Huh?" I turned around and looked at my dad. My mom was putting sunblock on herself, which meant she had stopped putting sunblock on me and I hadn't even **realized**!

"Did you hear what we said?" my mom asked, like I was not the world's best listener on Earth!

"Of course I heard you," I said, which was not really a lie. I *heard* them many times. I heard them earlier and yesterday and every day of my life!

"So you will be in charge of ordering room service for dinner?" Mom asked.

That would have been a good thing to hear if I had been listening.

"Yes! That is a very great idea. I will order certainly and apparently."

My parents gave very big *we love our Frannie* smiles.

"Great. Then it's a plan," my mom said.

Ordering **room service** for dinner was a very big job. I picked up the hotel book and studied the menu. There were so many things to order! Just when

I was going to ask their advice, my parents said they were going to take a dip. A *dip* is an expression adults use when they mean "going for a swim in the pool."

The waiter came back to collect our empty glasses.

"My mom said I could order room service for dinner!" I told him, because my **excitification** could not stay inside my mouth anymore.

"How exciting!" he said. "Would you like me to take the order?"

"But it's not dinnertime yet," I explained.

"That's okay. You can order anyway. We'll bring it to your room at the time you tell us."

"WOW. That is amazing," I told him.

When the waiter asked me, "So,

what would you like?" I got a **question mark** feeling in my stomach. *Are you one hundred percent sure you are supposed to order room service tonight?*

I looked at my parents in the pool and wondered whether I should wait for them to come out first. Just to check. But they looked like they were going to be in there for a very long time. Then the waiter said, "Why don't I come back?" and I got **scared he would forget** and never return.

"No! I know what to order," I told him.

I remembered that when my parents took me to a fancy restaurant named Balloo, the waiter told us about the specials. A *special* is when the chef at a restaurant makes a dish that's not usually on the menu. That's what makes it special!

"I will have the special," I told him.

"For how many?" he asked. That was a question I hadn't thought about. I counted the **number** of people who would be eating dinner: my mom, my dad, me, Henrietta's dad, and Henrietta.

"For five people," I told him.

"Five specials then?" he asked.

"Yes! For six thirty, room five seventeen. Thank you very much especially."

"You are very welcome."

When the waiter walked away, the question mark feeling came back for one half-second. I decided it wasn't about room service at all, but about meeting Henrietta! Because sometimes **wrong** and **nervous** feel the same.

CHAPTER

5

My mom said I had to take a shower before dressing up for dinner. We never dressed up for dinner at home because we weren't on business trips.

I went into my own bathroom and took a **short** shower because long ones waste water. I could not wait to see everyone's **impresstified** faces when room service came. Especially Henrietta, even though I didn't know what kind of face she had.

I put on an **important-looking** dress and my shiny shoes, combed my hair, and went into my parents' room.

"Oh, Frannie," my mom said. "You look so cute!"

"Adorable!" my dad added.

I scrunched up my face at them. Cute and adorable are kiddish.

"Sorry! I mean extremely fabulous," said my mom.

"Smashing!" my dad said.

I smiled. **Extremely fabulous** and **smashing** were much more adult.

"Thank you, and you look extremely fabulous and smashing as well!"

Just then there was a knock at our door and my dad and mom exchanged question mark looks. I did not know why they looked so **confusified**. I went to the door, opened it, and then gave the biggest *I cannot believe how amazing room service is and I wish that I had this in my very own home* gasp. There was a man in all white with two rolling tables that had a **hundredteen** covered silver platters on it.

"May I?" the waiter asked.

I could not even **speak**, so I just nodded and opened the door wider.

"What on earth?" my dad asked.

"Oh, this must be a huge mistake," my mom said to the waiter.

"No, it's not!" I said. "You told me I could order room service for dinner!"

My parents looked at each other and then back at me.

"When did we say that, Frannie?" my dad asked.

"At the pool. Mom said it."

"That is not what I said at all," my mom said in a voice that was a little bit **scoldish**.

My stomach filled up with **moths** and butterflies. "You didn't?"

"No." Then she turned to my dad. "Dan, did you hear me say Frannie could order room service tonight?"

"Nope, that's not what I heard at all. What I *did* hear was that *tomorrow*, after we all picked what we wanted off the menu, Frannie could call room service and place the order for the three of us," he said.

"Oh," I said. "I don't think my ears were turned on at the tomorrow part."

"No, Frances, clearly they were not," my mom said. When my parents Frances-ed me, I knew I was in a worldwide of trouble.

The room service man had taken all the lids off the platters and when they looked over, my parents each made the biggest gasps of the world.

"FRANCES!" my mother said loudly, putting both her hands over her mouth. Two Franceses in one conversation meant a double worldwide of trouble.

"Lobster?" my dad said, even louder than my mom's *Frances*. "You ordered"—then he counted—"FIVE lobsters??" His face was almost as red as the lobsters.

I knew the **lobster** part was bad because of all the Frances-ing, but I did not know exactly why.

"It was the special," I explained.

"What are we going to do with five *entire* lobsters?" my dad asked my mom.

"Why can't we just eat them?" I asked.

"Because we have dinner reservations with the Tilsons in the hotel restaurant."

The hotel restaurant?

"Oh," I said with a big gulp. Then I looked over at the waiter, who stood there holding the lids for the platters. All that food would now be wasted. I was not **exactly** sure what a person in a situation like this was supposed to do.

CHAPTER 6

If you don't already know this about lobsters or specials, they are usually the most **expensive** things on the menu. I learned this the hard way.

One other thing you might not know is that when your parents tell you something, you should turn your ears on. If you are not one hundred percent sure that your ears are turned on, you're **supposed to** ask them to repeat their words.

My dad tried to talk the waiter out of everything. He said it had been a big mistake, and I hadn't been listening, and that he was **very, very sorry**.

The room service man was certainly nice, even when he was giving us the bad news of the world. The lobsters had already been cooked which was a for instance of why we had to pay for the most expensive thing on the menu. Five times, as a matter of fact.

My dad and mom tried **everything** they could to make this problem go away, but the waiter said there was nothing he could do about it.

"But we're meeting people for dinner in the dining room. We're late, actually," said my dad.

"I'm sorry, sir. I don't know what to tell you," the waiter said. And that's when I had the most **geniusal** idea on the planet of earth.

"Mom, isn't that stuff you buy in the summertime called lobster salad?"

"Lobster salad?" she asked. "What about it?"

"What if we put the lobsters in the refrigerator for right now and then we made lobster salad with them. We could eat it tomorrow."

My parents looked at each other.

"That's not a bad idea actually," my dad said.

"We could have a picnic at Princessland!" I suggested. "That way, we won't spend any more money actually!"

My dad looked at me with a look that said *Frannie, you are a genius of the earth.* **However and nevertheless**, we still had more problems to solve.

"Who exactly is going to *make* the lobster salad?" asked my dad, looking straight into my eyeballs.

I looked over at the lobsters and scrunched up my face at that question. Their antennas were so . . . antennas-ish. Their little, black eyes were so . . . black eyes-ish. But I knew the answer.

"Me?" I asked my dad.

"Yes, exactly. You."

"And what about the mayonnaise, celery, pepper, and lemon juice that we'll need to make the salad?" asked my mother, also looking right into my eyeballs.

"Does your kitchen have those ingredients?" I asked the waiter.

"Of course!" he answered.

The moths and butterflies in my stomach were starting to calm down. "Can we borrow them?"

"I think that can be arranged," he said.

I looked at my parents with a big grin. "Solved!"

"Fantastic," my dad said. "Now, please help us put everything in the refrigerator, and then you can help"—my dad looked at the waiter's name tag—"Clark put the lids back on all the platters."

My face almost fell off my head. All that was going to take a pamillionteen hours! I wanted to meet Henrietta already! But my dad's face said *I am not joking, Frannie. Not even for a centimeter of a second.*

After helping to put the stuff away, we all left to meet the Henriettas.

"Are you still mad at me?" I asked my mom in the elevator.

"I'm a little cross," she said.

"Oh," I said as all my worries gathered up in my stomach. I do not like when my mom is cross because it lasts longer than angry.

Then my dad added, "We're going to have a good, long talk after dinner tonight, all right, Frannie?"

I looked down at the floor and took my mom's hand.

"Okay," I said. I did not like good, long talks. Good, long talks are the ones we have whenever I'm in trouble with the law. And when you're in trouble with the law that means your parents are *really* cross at you.

I knew they still loved me, though, because they let me press the elevator button for *R. R* is the floor where the hotel restaurant is and pressing it is something they knew I would prefer. (Prefer is a word that grown-ups use. It is a way to fancy up *something that you like better. Like* is a kid word and that is why I prefer *prefer*.) I had planned to let go of my mom's hand once we got inside the restaurant, but that plan did not work. My hand was very **overwhelmified** by the hotel restaurant. I could not even believe my eye sockets about how **gigantoristic** it was.

Once I got used to how many tables there were (probably eighteen thousand), I noticed actually that it was my favorite kind of restaurant. It was the **buffet** kind! At a buffet, you can put exactly what you want on your plate. There were about eighty-hundred buffet areas. It was a good thing that the word *buffet* means you can go back as many times as you want.

"There they are," my dad said as he walked toward a man and one very regular-looking kid. All my excitement dried right up. Henrietta wasn't fancy at all. All she wore was a pair of white jeans and a T-shirt. I felt a little bit standout-ish in my **dress**. I wished my mother hadn't told me to dress up, but since I was in trouble with the law, I didn't say anything about it.

I noticed that Henrietta's T-shirt said "California Girl" on it. That gave me an idea to make a shirt like that for myself that said "Chester Girl."

"You must be Frannie," Mr. Henrietta said. "I'm Fred Tilson."

"Hi, Fred Tilson," I said. When you repeat someone's name after they say it, you will **never** forget it, ever.

"This is Henry," Fred Tilson said. I put my hand out to shake, but Henrietta just waved and said, "Hey," like someone woke her up in the middle of the night and made her talk. I did not appreciate that her hello to me was **in a bad mood**. But I did like that her nickname was Henry. I'd never met **a girl with a boy's name** before.

"You can call me Frankly," I told them.

Henry's name sounded sort of **professional** to me, so I decided I was going to use my professional name also.

Fred Tilson smiled and said, "Frankly it is."

When we sat down I noticed that Henry's grumpy was not just about her hello. Her grumpy was about **everything!**

"Do you want some bread, Henry?" Fred Tilson asked.

"No!" She snapped at him like he offered her **poison balls** and not delicious restaurant rolls.

"How about a breadstick then? You just told me you were starving," Fred Tilson said.

"No," she said again, crossing her arms and turning her head away from him.

"Maybe it would be fun to talk about Princessland and what rides you girls might want to go on," my mom said. My mom is very **smart** about bad moods and **changing the subject**.

Henry and Fred Tilson exchanged looks, and then he turned to us and said, "I'm afraid we have some bad news."

"Oh no," my mom said, worried.

"I'm sorry to say that Henry isn't going to be able to join you tomorrow."

Henry crossed her arms even harder.

"Why not?" I asked.

"It turns out that we're short a couple of helpers. So I need Henry to work at the conference tomorrow. I'm hoping one helper will be enough."

Helpers? Work? Conference? These were some of my **favorite** words in the world.

Except for conference. I had no idea what that meant.

I looked up at my dad, and he knew me so well, he read my question right from my **brain**.

"Tomorrow Mr. Tilson and I are going to a big meeting with all of our co-workers. There will be different speakers throughout the day. The speakers talk to us about subjects we're all interested in. That meeting is called a conference."

A conference sounded great! I wanted to go to a conference! I had twenty-three eighteen interests!

"Mr. Tilson and I happen to have arranged this particular conference," my father explained.

I stood up.

"You're in *charge* of the conference?" I asked.

He smiled. "And so is Mr. Tilson."

"You're the BOSSES of the conference?" I asked again. I could not believe my own father was the actual boss of a real, live conference.

He and Fred Tilson laughed, but Henry did not.

"We are both the bosses of the conference," my dad told me.

"I'm glad that you're so impressed," Fred Tilson said.

I sat back down and looked at them both with **brand-new eyes**. "I am very impresstified," I said. "Very impresstified, indeed."

That's when I realized something that made my stomach fill with butterflies and moths. If Fred Tilson and my dad were the bosses of the conference, and Henrietta got to help them, then they all had jobs and I didn't. Why couldn't *I* help tomorrow? Why did Henrietta get to have all the **fun**?

"How long is the conference?" I asked.

"Just one day. It will be over by five o'clock."

I was so jealous of Henry. I pictured her running around looking

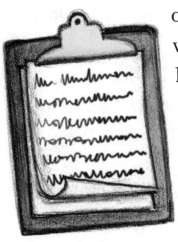

official and important with a **clipboard** in her hands. Maybe she'd get to wear a uniform! Maybe an HH shirt. Maybe they'd even give her an office!

I probably knew much more about clipboards and **office supplies** than Henry. What if Henry didn't know what to do with all of that? I'd be at Princessland and she might need someone like me to help her and explain official business conference things! I worried that the tears that were forming behind my eyes would decide to come out.

"It's so unfair," Henry said. "Why does Frankly get to go to

Princessland and I have to stay here at the dumb hotel and work at a stupid conference?"

"It's just one day, Henry," her dad said. "It's not going to hurt you."

"It is to! It is going to hurt me!" Henry pouted.

Henry wasn't fancy, but she was very **dramatical**. She turned to me. "You are so lucky, Frankly. You get to go to Princessland and I have to go to work!"

I did not want to tell her that I thought *she* was the lucky one. After all, she seemed very **grumpified** about having to work in the first place.

"There is nothing worse than work!" Henry said loudly.

That was not a scientific fact. I was getting a little **angrified** that she was saying bad things about jobs. Especially since my dad and her dad were the bosses of the exact job she was yelling about.

"I've had jobs before actually," I told Henry. "I *like* working."

I didn't care if she made fun of me. People should not be mad at things they haven't even tried before! Like **delicious restaurant rolls** and jobs!

"What kind of jobs?" Henry asked me, clearly impresstified.

"A food critic, a waitress, and a radio announcer," I told her. "I'm very workerish." That's when I remembered I had my **business cards** on me. My dad already had one, but Fred Tilson didn't. I could run upstairs and get my résumé, too. That way, he could hire me, also! Or, maybe

I could switch places with Henry. I could work at the conference and she could go to Princessland. But then she'd be with my mom and I wanted to be with my mom! This was the most frustrating kind of problem.

Out of my eye edge I saw my mom give a **tiny** worried look to my dad. My mom was so excited about tomorrow's visit to Princessland because that's where she went when she was my age. She was really looking forward to a ride called **teacups**. It's like a merry-go-round but you sit in giant teacups that spin.

I could not disappoint my mom. I did not like when she was sick and I did not like when she gave me worried looks. Those were the two worst things in the entire world. But I *really,*

really, really, really, really wanted to work at the conference. Henry was the **luckiest** person I'd ever met in my life that day.

After dinner we made the lobster salad. It was one of the hardest things I've ever tried to do. My hands broke trying to crack the lobster shells open and my eyeballs broke from having to look at the lobsters' **horrendifying** intestines which were even worser than the **tentacles** and **eyes**. The whole thing took four hundredteen hours to do and that is not an opinion.

It is also not an opinion that I will never order lobster from room service again.

After I brushed my teeth and got ready for bed, my parents tucked me in—one person at a time starting with my dad.

"Your mom and I are really enjoying having you here in Florida with us," he said.

"Thanks, Dad," I said. But I knew for a scientific fact there was a *but* coming.

"But . . . ," he said.

See what I mean about *but*?

"I'm still upset about the lobsters. You know about double-checking when you're not one hundred percent sure about something we said," he told me.

"But I WAS sure mom said I could order dinner," I told him.

"One hundred percent sure?"

"Well, maybe not one hundred percent."

"Maybe now that you've made the lobster salad, you'll have an easier time remembering to be one hundred percent sure in the future."

"Probably," I said. Then I sat up. "Dad?" I asked. There was something I *was* **one hundred percent** sure about and that was that I wanted to work at his **conference** tomorrow. And I was going to tell him.

"Yes?"

"Tomorrow—," I started, and then looked up to see my mom standing in the doorway smiling and waiting her turn to say good night.

"Yes?"

I wanted to say it so badly. But I

couldn't. I could not hurt my mom's feelings.

"Tomorrow is going to be a great day," I said.

"I certainly hope so," he said, kissing me on the head.

Then my mom sat down on my bed and told me about all the different types of things we were going to do at Princessland. She could **hardly** even wait to get there. She was going to take me on all the rides her mom took her on. She especially couldn't **wait** to ride the teacups with me. She hoped I loved them as much as she did.

I knew I was going to have to do the grown-up thing and pretend there was no conference. After all, I have a really good imagination. So tomorrow, when I saw Henry with her clipboard and my dad being a boss with Fred Tilson, I'd just pretend they were doing something else. Something I would never want to do. Not ever.

Like making **lobster salad**.

CHAPTER

The next morning at breakfast my mom had a big **Princessland smile** on her face while she read the newspaper. Any time a conference thought **tickled** my brain, I was going to look at her.

But I was not going to think about the conference.

Not once.

Not even for one **sip** of water.

Or when my dad pulled conference-looking paper out of his briefcase and highlighted a lot of words with an orange marker.

I wasn't even going to look.

"What is that, Dad?" I asked, only looking a little bit.

"It's a schedule of all the events today. Do you want to see?"

I nodded yes, and he handed me the **stapled paper**. I didn't understand what it said, but I felt so professional holding it in my hands. I really wanted to keep it. I decided it was okay to think about the **conference** just for a couple of minutes.

"Don't throw this out, okay?"

"I promise. I won't."

"Or the highlighter."

"It's a deal."

"Do you get other paper things at a conference?"

"Yes, actually. I'll probably get some pamphlets and brochures and a name badge."

My face almost fell off into my cereal bowl. I have **always** wanted a name badge that had my name on it and that is not an opinion.

"Tell you what," Dad began. "You can have all my conference materials when I'm done. How's that sound?"

"Fantastical!" I smiled. Now I couldn't wait for the conference to be over so I could have all of my dad's really workerish and official materials. I could certainly use them when I had **conferences in my room** with my best friend, Elliott.

"Do you think that there will be enough people to help out today?" I asked.

"I hope so," my dad said, a little distractified with his pages and official highlighting pen. A co-worker waved at him from across the room. My dad was so lucky to have so many co-workers! I didn't even have one!

"Because Fred Tilson said that they didn't have enough helpers, so I was just curious about that. That is the only reason I am asking. I am not asking for any other reason in particular," I said.

My dad motioned to the waiter for more coffee. My mother lowered her newspaper and looked over at me. Then she raised it back up and kept reading.

"Don't you worry about that, Birdy," my dad said. "You just concentrate on your own job."

I sat up, excited. "*My own* job?" I asked. "I have a job?"

"Your job is to have fun with Mom, of course," he said, like I was being silly that I didn't even know what my own job was!

I scrunched up my face at him, but he was too distractified with his really special conference papers. **It is a scientific fact that having fun at Princessland is *not* a job.** Princessland is not a jobs kind of a place. Princessland is a *rides* kind of place. But do you know what *is* a **jobs** kind of place?

A conference!

"Henry has never had a job before, so I'm worried she might break the conference. I'm sure no one would prefer that," I told him.

"I'm sure she'll do just fine," my mom said.

"I hope so," I told her. "I really do, because Henry was really complainy. So that's what I'm really worried about. It's a good thing she doesn't have a very important type of job," I said.

"Actually," my dad said, "she's in charge of name badges. That's a big responsibility."

BADGES!? She was in charge of

badges?! I could not even believe my ears about this news.

Just then, my dad looked at his watch.

"I have about ten more minutes before I have to go meet Tina Zucker."

"Who's Tina Zucker?" I asked.

"She's the guest speaker."

"Guest speaker?" I had never heard of this job before. It **certainly** sounded very important.

"A guest speaker is the person who makes a speech. She'll welcome everybody to the conference and get them thinking about some of the topics of the day," my dad explained.

"What kind of topics?"

"Something you are already very

good at," my dad said. "Creativity in the work place—how to use your imagination to help you do a better job."

"They have conferences about that?" I asked. I did not know that being **creative** was a conference kind of topic. If I had known that all along, I would have asked to be the **guest speaker**!

A waiter came over and refilled our water glasses.

"Mrs. Pellington says I have a *simply magnificent* imagination!" I told them.

"And you most certainly do," my mom agreed.

"Maybe if the guest speaker doesn't have a good idea for a speech, she could call me on Mom's cell phone while we're at Princessland."

"I'll certainly let her know," my dad

said. "But she's one of the very best guest speakers—"

"Or we can just wait until she gets here, and I can give her some good ideas myself. Or even just my business card," I interrupted. Turning to my mother **so she wouldn't feel bad**, I said, "And *then* we can go to Princessland."

"I think she probably has some good ideas, Birdy. I wouldn't worry about it."

"In fact," I added, "if anyone seems to need help with anything whatsoever, they can just call me on Mom's cell phone and I can tell them how to use all the office supplies."

My mom looked at me for **a long time**.

"Frannie?"

"Yes?"

"Would you prefer to stay here instead of going to Princessland today?"

I didn't say anything because I was still worried I would hurt her feelings.

"It's okay if you do," she said with a voice that had only a tiny bit of sadness in it.

"Well, kind of," I said.

"You really want to be cooped up inside all day in dark rooms with no windows when we're here in sunny, beautiful Florida?" my dad asked me.

"It's beautiful in here, too!" I said.

My parents laughed. Then they looked at each other.

"I thought we would spread Princessland over two days, but I guess just going tomorrow is good enough," my mom told my dad.

"I don't see why not," he said.

Then they looked at me.

"Frannie?" my mom asked in a very top-level business type of voice. I sat up really tall.

"Yes, mom?"

"I want to make sure that your father and I understand. You would *prefer* to stay inside today and work, is that correct?"

"Yes!"

"On a spectacularly and utterly cloud-free, beautiful day, you would rather be inside this hotel than at Princessland?"

I stood up so excited. "Yes, yes, yes, yes, yes!" I cried. Then people at other tables turned around to look at me, so I sat down again.

"Yes," I whispered one more time for good luck.

"You really are something else, Frannie," my mom said with **a lot of hugs** in her voice.

"You're the only child I know who'd rather work than play," my dad said.

I shrugged. "That's just the kind of person I prefer to be."

"I want you to have a wonderful time on this trip, Frannie. But I think that it's only fair that we compromise," my mom said.

"Okay, what is the compromise?" I asked.

"The compromise is that today you can help Henry with her job, but tomorrow we are going to Princessland! No if, ands, or buts!"

"That's a really good compromise," I told my mom.

"Great. It's all settled. Should we

go find Henry and give her the good news?" my mom asked.

I jumped up out of my seat.

"Yes! Let's go!"

We collected all of our things and then we went to find Henry so I could start my **official job** of the day!

CHAPTER

My parents walked me to the help desk where **Henry and Fred Tilson** stood.

"Looks like you'll have some company today," my dad said to Henry. "Frannie is going to help you."

"Frankly," I corrected him, with my professional voice.

"They won't let you go to Princessland, either?" Henry asked in her grumpy voice.

"We're going to go tomorrow," I told her.

"That's when my dad and I are going!" she said. "But until then, we have to work at a stupid job."

"Well, the good news, Henry, is that I'm putting you in charge," my dad said. I looked up at him with an *is that a scientific fact* question mark face.

"You are?" Henry asked suddenly, a little bit excited.

"Yes. You're older. You can keep an eye on Frannie."

"Frankly," I said again.

"Sorry. Frankly," he corrected.

I did not prefer the part about Henry keeping her eyes on me. My eyes were much more professional. Even if they were younger.

Fred Tilson explained our jobs to

us. I turned my ears on so that I would be one hundred percent sure I heard everything he said. I did not want to have another **room service accident**.

"You will sit behind the badges, which are in alphabetical order."

I am one of the best alphabetical orderers I've ever met, and that is not an opinion. This thought filled me with **pride-itity** because I already knew I would be apparently very good at this job.

"If they get out of alphabetical order, I am really good at putting them back how they were," I told Fred Tilson. This was information he needed to know. In case he made me **boss of badges**.

"Let's not touch the badges, okay?" Fred Tilson said. That did not give me a very good day feeling on my skin. Touching the badges would be the best part of the job!

"The badges are only for the conference goers. Let the adults find their names for themselves, okay?"

Henry and I nodded, but I did not agree with his "okay"—not one bit.

"I want you both to stay at that table until every last badge has been claimed. Okay? Not one badge should go unattended."

We nodded and followed Fred Tilson to the table we would sit at and never leave until all the badges were gone. When we got there, Fred Tilson got a big box out from

AIR EXPRESS

under the table. It was white with the words "Air Express" on it and had a picture of an airplane.

"What's that?" I asked.

"Henry is going to make sure that Tina Zucker gets that box when she comes in," said Fred Tilson.

I **stepped forward**. "I have a lot of experience with boxes, Mr. Tilson. I will make sure that Tina Zucker gets the box."

"Thank you, Frankly. I think Henry has it under control."

"A for instance of what I mean is that whenever my parents want to put things in the basement, they put it in a box and carry it down. So I know a lot about that."

"You may absolutely help Henry keep an eye on the box because there are extremely important papers in there."

This is when all my skin almost jumped off me to hug Fred Tilson. I LOVE important papers!

"What kind of important papers?" I asked.

"Mrs. Zucker sent her speech ahead of time just to make sure she wouldn't lose it. There are also handouts for the audience. I suppose there are pencils in there, too," he said. But before I had the chance to discuss **my experience with pencils**, Fred Tilson wished us good luck and walked away to do his own job somewhere else.

I looked at Henry, whose eyeballs were not nearly as workerish as mine. In fact, after we sat down in our professional chairs, she started to doodle on a blank badge. Since **I was not the boss of her**, I could not say *Names go on badges, not doodles!* Which is a for instance of something I would say if I were the boss of her.

The badges were **very beautiful**. The names were typed with real, typed letters and not handwritten ones, like the badges I make at home. They were laid out in perfectly **straight rows**. Except for one tricky row that was a little bit crooked and needed to be fixed.

"What are you doing?" Henry asked, looking up.

"Just uncrookeding the badges," I told her.

"We're not supposed to touch anything," she told me.

"It's okay," I told her. I wasn't

changing anything, just fixing something, so it could not have been against the law.

I reached out to line up the **M** badges a little bit straighter, and that's when I noticed the best **surprise** of ever! You will not even believe your ears about this.

MY NAME WAS ON ONE OF THE BADGES!

Well, *almost* my name. They just accidentally put FRANCESCA MILLER instead of FRANCES MILLER. But I knew what they meant, so it was really okay.

When I picked up the badge, I noticed it was the **real** kind. The kind you pin to your shirt, which is what I did.

Henry looked up and bossed, "You're not allowed to do that."

"It's okay," I told her. "It has my name on it." I felt bad that they forgot to make Henry one, but the badge makers probably **knew** I had had jobs before.

"Francesca is the long name for Frannie?" Henry asked me.

"Sometimes," I told her. "But mine is Frances."

That's when I wondered just a **centimeter** whether this really *was* my badge since I wasn't even supposed

to be here at all. And also since it wasn't my *exact* name. But who else's could it have been?

Henry shrugged and continued drawing, and I sat and waited as patiently as I could. Finally our first customer came! I knew he was a top-level person because he was wearing **a bow tie**. I stood up and held my hand out for him to shake, but he was too busy looking at the badges.

"Hello, sir. Can I help you find your name?"

"I got it, thanks," he said, scanning the table and picking up the badge with his name: ED STERN.

Soon, other people started coming in. Everyone was moving very quickly and no one asked for help! That's why I decided to stand **closer** to the front of the table. Then everyone would understand that I was **a worker**.

At three badges left, a very tall woman came in, but didn't see her name.

"Do you need help?" I asked her.

"Yes," she said, a little bit crossishly. This gave me a bad day feeling on my skin. "Where's Mr. Tilson or Mr. Miller?" she asked me in a very angrified way.

"I'll find them," Henry said as she got up and ran as fast as possible. The lady crossed her arms and watched

Henry run across the hotel lobby. When Henry came back, Fred Tilson was with her.

"Fran?" he asked. "Is everything okay?"

"There's no badge for me," she said.

"Of course there is! I saw it myself," he said, walking to the table. Fran and I followed him and the three of us **stared** at the badges. Even though I didn't know Fran's entire name, I looked, anyway.

"That's strange," Mr. Tilson said, looking at all the names.

He turned to Henry. "Did you see a badge that said FRANCESCA MILLER?"

Uh-oh.

Henry looked **straight** at the badge that was pinned to me, and then so did Fred Tilson and Francesca Miller.

"Frannie! What are you doing wearing that?" he asked me, sounding scoldish. "Please give Mrs. Miller her badge."

I looked down at my chest.

"I'm sorry. I thought it was for me," I told them.

"The instructions were not to touch anything," Fred Tilson said.

I unpinned the badge and handed it to Fran.

"Our names are almost the same," I told her. "My name is Frances Miller. That's why I got confused."

"An honest mistake then," she said as she pinned my almost name to her shirt. She did not smile, though, and it is a scientific fact that you *can* smile at "honest mistakes."

Then I got a great idea. I reached

into my pocket and pulled out my gold pilot wings.

"Do you want to wear this for a little while?" I asked. "That way you can wear something of mine like I wore something of yours!"

She looked down at the gold wings and smiled. "That's very sweet of you to offer, but I think you should hold on to the wings." I was very **proud of myself** for being so smart about getting her to smile.

After Fred Tilson told her what room to go to, he told me I was getting a new job. My ears did not like that **sentence**.

Fred Tilson moved the box from under the badge table to a chair in the corner. "I want you to sit right here. Don't move," he said, pushing the box a little under the chair. "When Mrs. Zucker comes, make sure she gets this box. All you need to do is point to it. Do not touch it. Okay? It's very easy."

I nodded as I sat down. Then I realized something. "How will I know it's her? I've never met Mrs. Zucker before," I told him.

"She looks like a ballerina, actually. She's very tall and graceful with black hair always pulled back in a bun." Then he went off with his co-workers.

I couldn't wait until Mrs. Zucker walked through the doors. I'd point to the box and show Fred Tilson what a **great worker** I am after all. And then next year, I'd get to be the boss of Henry!

But that's not what happened.

Not even at all.

CHAPTER

I waited for six hundred years for Tina Zucker, but she never came! It was probably **already tomorrow**! My legs were getting bored.

When I looked over at Henry to see what she was doing, she wasn't there! I couldn't believe it! There was still one badge left! We were not **supposed** to leave the table until everyone had their badges! And I was not supposed to leave my chair until Mrs. Zucker had her box!

This was a **true emergency**. The kind of emergency that needed very quick attention! Maybe there was a way for me to do both Henry's job and my own. If I sat where Henry had been, then I could still see the box. That way, when Mrs. Zucker came in, I could point to the box from the badge table, like Fred Tilson said. *Oh, Frannie*, I thought. *You are a genius of the earth.*

When I sat down at the table, I stared right at the box under the chair. Suddenly a worry flew into my brain. What if the reason Henry wasn't here was because she quit! That was probably it! She was probably upset that Fred Tilson gave me her **box-watching job**! I had to fix things right away.

Uh-oh! I looked over at the hotel lobby and saw Henry talking to her dad. Oh no, she *was* quitting! I had to get her to un-quit. If I did that in front of Fred Tilson, then he would love me so much and forgive me for my big, bad badge mistake!

I tried waving to Henry, but she didn't see me. I had no choice but to run over to her. But when I was halfway there, her dad left and Henry turned around and started walking toward me. A big disappointment puddle fell at my feet that I'd missed my big chance.

"Did you quit your job?" I asked as she came near me.

"No," she said. "My dad was showing me where Mrs. Zucker will give her speech."

"Oh," I said, feeling a little sad that I did not get to save the day. As soon

as I sat back down in my chair, the front
doors opened and a very late–looking
woman ran in. She had black hair, but
it was not in a bun. It was loose and
wild, and she was rushing all over
the place. She didn't look like any
ballerina I ever saw, but I knew it was
Tina Zucker.

I looked down at the box and got my
finger ready to point. And that's when
my heart breathed extra hard and I
gasped the biggest gasp of ever. When
I looked down at the box, I realized
that I wasn't forgetting anything; I
was missing something. The box! It
was **gone**!

CHAPTER 10

Everything seemed to happen very slowly and very quickly at the same time. Mrs. Zucker and Henry both turned to me. Henry was pointing her finger at me. As Mrs. Zucker started to walk in my direction, I **froze** like **an ice cube**. That's how shocktified I felt.

"Are you Frannie? Do you have my box?" Mrs. Zucker was standing right over me.

Just when I opened my mouth to tell her the bad news, a smile broke onto my face. "There it is!" I cried and ran over to a table that said MAIL TABLE. It had lots of envelopes and boxes on it, including Mrs. Zucker's Air Express box.

Mrs. Zucker rushed over and picked it up, and then Henry led us up the stage and through the curtains to the backstage area. Mrs. Zucker put the box down and then hurried onstage. She must have been a real professional because she knew exactly how to use the microphone and everything.

"Hi, everyone. I am so sorry to keep you all waiting. I had a disastrous flight. First, my plane was delayed, then my baggage was lost, then my car never came, and then the bus stalled! I was afraid I was going to have to give my speech from the highway!"

The audience laughed and I thought to myself, *Wow—Mrs. Zucker is the best guest speaker I've ever heard in my worldwide life!*

Then she started talking about some things that were **business-ish** and said something about the box and how Henry and I were going to hand out some papers in a minute. That's when she turned to us and called out, "Girls, will you open that box and bring me my speech and those papers?"

We opened the box and that is when I noticed the most horrible truth of the world. There weren't any papers in the box at all! What *was* in the box exactly were juggling pins. I didn't know what they were doing there. **Juggling pins** are not very **conference-ish**.

"Where are the papers?" Henry asked me.

"I don't know!" I said, and then I got a really bad day feeling on my skin when I realized something **worse than horrible**. Not only was this the wrong box, I didn't know where the right one was!

"Let's hurry up now, girls," Mrs. Zucker said into the microphone. It was the most humilifying moment.

"What should we do?" Henry asked me.

"I don't know!" I told her. "You're the boss!"

"I guess this is taking longer than expected," Mrs. Zucker said. "My speech is in the box. If I could remember my speech, I'd start giving it, but, of course, I don't." The audience was very quiet and I heard people **fidgeting**.

Fidgeting is a very bad sign because that's what people do when they are not paying attention. This is a scientific fact. My teacher, Mrs. Pellington, tells us this all the time.

"Frannie, what's going on?" I heard an angry voice ask. My father's angry voice as a matter of fact and nevertheless.

I tried to think of an answer that was **truth-telling**, but also please-do-not-get-one-more-inch-mad-at-me sounding. But I couldn't think that quickly. "The box doesn't have Mrs. Zucker's papers in it. Only juggling pins," I told him. His face turned as

bright orange as the highlighter he
had used at breakfast.

When he was at his **most orange**,
Henry said she'd go looking for the box.
I did not prefer to be left alone with my
father at that exact moment actually.

"How could you have let this
happen? Weren't you supposed to
be watching the box?" he asked, his
voice channel still on angry.

Before I could even answer, he
jumped off the stage and ran toward
a door that Henry and I didn't even
know about! It was all the way on the
opposite side of the auditorium.

"Where's everyone running off to?"
Mrs. Zucker asked again.

Just when I thought my life was
ruined forever, I got the idea to
dump some of the pins out and see if

maybe the papers were underneath everything!

"Um . . . one minute," I shouted as I took out a bunch of pins. My brain started to **wonder** who the pins belonged to and whether someone else was in trouble for losing a box.

That's when Mrs. Zucker made a noise into the microphone that sounded a little bit like a **giggle**. But what was happening wasn't funny, so it couldn't have been. Except then I heard it again. I stopped pulling pins out of the box and looked up.

"Excuse me," Mrs. Zucker said. "Sometimes when I'm nervous I start to—" She stopped and bent over in a laughing fit. Her shoulders bobbed **up** and **down**. Uh-oh. I really hoped someone would find the right box.

Mrs. Zucker stepped away from the microphone for a moment. Then she came back.

"Okay, I'm better. Now, where was—" And then it started all over again!

Finally Henry came back, but with no box. "Did something funny happen?" she asked.

I shook my head no. "She just started laughing and won't stop."

"Okay, sorry again," Mrs. Zucker said into the microphone. "I'm better now. I got all the giggles out. I promise."

Then the audience giggled **a little bit** and Mrs. Zucker turned to us again.

"Girls, help me out here, would ya? My speech?"

That's when I knew I had to tell her what was happening. I waved her over.

"Excuse me for one second," she said into the microphone and headed toward me.

"What is going on?" she asked.

My mouth was very dry, almost like I had an entire **beach of sand** in there.

"We have the wrong box," I told her.

"What do you mean?" She looked at the box and saw all the pins on the ground.

"Oh, for goodness' sake!" she snapped. "I can't believe this. How hard is it to keep track of one box?" Then she stormed back to the microphone.

"It seems the girls who were supposed to keep an eye on my box ended up losing it."

I was completely **humilified**.

CHAPTER

Even though Mrs. Zucker couldn't remember her speech, she said she'd **try**. But her try sounded like this:

"How to describe imagination? Imagine if your brain opened up and . . . oh goodness . . . I can't remember . . ."

She was sweating a lot and clearing her throat. I could hear a lot of people in the audience coughing and I saw two people **leave**! It was becoming the most **gigantoristic** moment of awful I'd ever seen.

Then, just when things could not get any worse, they did. Mrs. Zucker's microphone went dead. She tapped on it, leaned in, and asked, "Hello? Can you hear me?" A couple people yelled, "No!"

"Oh, for goodness' sake! What a mess!" Mrs. Zucker pulled a handkerchief out of her pocket and wiped her face. She took the microphone out of its holder and hit it again and again, but there was no sound. Then, holding the microphone, she turned to us, and Henry called out, "I'll get help!"

She was very fast and came back quickly with a **microphone man**. That is a for instance of a man who fixes microphones. He took it from

Mrs. Zucker and handed it to Henry to hold.

I scrunched my face at her because I was jealous. I wanted to hold something, too!

Mrs. Zucker was yelling so that people could hear her **bad-memory speech**. It is not an opinion that her speech was not a good one. She wasn't even saying anything about imagination that was very **true**. A for instance of what I mean is that her speech sounded like this:

"Sometimes we get stuck, but we need to really concentrate. Because we have a deadline. So . . . uh . . . how do we focus? We . . . well, we stretch in our chairs or we pace in our office or we . . . um"—Mrs. Zucker looked in our direction and then back at the audience—"sometimes I just shut my eyes and repeat a word . . ."

Henry **rolled** her **eyeballs** about the speech, and I leaned over and said, "This is the most boringest speech in America!"

And you would never guess what happened no matter how hard you tried.

As those exact words came spilling out of my mouth, the microphone started to work again. A for instance of what I mean is that everyone heard me call Mrs. Zucker's speech **boring**!

Henry's mouth dropped off her face. I looked over at the microphone man who stood up and smiled.

"I guess it's fixed," he said.

That is when I felt my entire body turn the color of beets. I looked out at the audience. A lot of people were whispering and some people in the front row looked embarrassed like they were the ones to have said the awful thing and not me. My skin burned up with **humilification** when I realized that it wasn't just the audience who heard me. I turned to Mrs. Zucker. She was staring right at me with the most **hurtish** kind of face. There was so much quiet everywhere I bet if I had really tried, I could have heard my own hair growing.

It was the worst moment of my entire life. The only lucky part was that my dad hadn't heard me because he was still outside the auditorium looking for the box. But **Mr. Tilson was there**, and he looked angry enough for himself and my dad put together.

I wanted to turn the color invisible. I was very afraid that Mrs. Zucker was going to yell at me in front of the whole conference of America. And I felt **horrendimous** times twenty millionteen for making her feel bad.

If someone called me boring in front of a room full of people, I would cry until there were no tears left behind my eyeballs, and then I'd drink a machillion more gallons of water so I could cry some more. It was the kind of moment where you wished it was **any** other moment in the whole worldwide of other moments.

I opened my mouth to push a sorry out, but before I could even make a sound, Mrs. Zucker tried to say something and then just started laughing again! She laughed so hard, she had to sit down on a nearby chair. This made me confused, but also a little relieved. I looked at the audience and they seemed a little **relieviated**, too.

Then, from the chair, she announced, "I can do this!" and walked back to the microphone. But the second she got there, she burst into laughter again, and then she started crying. But it wasn't a sad kind of crying. It was **a laughing kind of crying**. Henry gave me a *what should we do?* kind of face. Then she grabbed my hand and pulled me out onstage.

"Do you need our help?" Henry asked Mrs. Zucker.

Still giggling, Mrs. Zucker pointed at me. "She said my speech was boring. Right into the microphone!"

"I'm really, really, really, sorry," I said. "Really, really."

Mrs. Zucker's laughing started to calm down a little.

She took a couple of deep breaths. Henry and I stood there gripping each other's hands.

Then Mrs. Zucker looked at me. "What was boring about my speech?"

I couldn't believe my ears were hearing this question. Everyone was staring at me and the hot lights were shining down on my head. Did Mrs. Zucker want me to hurt her feelings again? Then I thought maybe **she liked getting her feelings hurt because it made her laugh**.

"Well, I don't think stretching and stuff is very imaginationary."

"It's not. It's just a way to get your ideas flowing."

"I just don't think that it's the *best* way," I explained.

"Well, what would you say *is* the best way to come up with creative ideas?" she asked.

"Well, I don't exactly *come up* with them. They sort of . . . come up to me."

Mrs. Zucker tilted her head to the side, which meant she was **a little interested**. "What do you mean?" she asked.

"Like when I am doing *one* thing, that's when I get my geniusal ideas for *other* things."

"You mean you come up with your best ideas when you're not trying to come up with your best ideas?"

"Yes!" I said. "That's it exactly! Like one time when I was drawing hopscotch boxes in chalk, I came up with the idea for coloring book wallpaper! And another time when I was washing the dishes with my dad, I came up with the geniusal idea for how to recycle newspapers and magazines."

Someone in the audience raised their hand and Mrs. Zucker called on her. It was a lady with **bright red hair** and she called out, "Do you think getting out of the office and taking a walk might be helpful?" I looked at

Mrs. Zucker who said, "I think that question is for you."

For me? WOW. I couldn't believe **a real, live audience** person was asking me a question!

"Yes, I think that is a spectaculary idea. It is best if you do something completely different because then your brain will be homesick for the thing you're not thinking about and go back to it all on its own!" I explained.

The audience made noises like it liked that answer.

"Do you think you could give us another example?" Mrs. Zucker asked me.

"Sure!" I said. "I could give you a hundreteen examples."

"Just one more for now would be fine," Mrs. Zucker said.

I put **my thinking face** on and came up with the most perfectish example.

"Well, one time I decided to see how things looked through squinted eyes. And I saw a sign that said, 'Christmases for Sale,' but when I unsquinted I saw that it really said, 'Mattresses for Sale.' Then I got the idea to write a story about a store that sold Christmases. All because of squinting!" I knew this example was a little different from the other two examples I gave, but it was also the same because I wasn't *trying* to think of a story about Christmases for sale.

"Frannie, thank you so much," Mrs. Zucker said. "Those were great examples, and very helpful, too. Right?" she asked the audience.

"YES!" a couple people yelled. Then

Mrs. Zucker told everyone they should give me a round of applause, which meant that everyone clapped for me and **some people even stood up**! That is when I decided to bow. I could not even believe how good it felt to be a guest speaker!

Then Mrs. Zucker said some last words to everyone, which sounded very smart, but were a little **too fancy for my ears**. When she was done, she thanked me for giving everyone such great ideas. Then everyone clapped again, and it sounded like they were clapping even harder than before.

When we saw that a lot of people from the audience were coming up to the stage to talk to Mrs. Zucker, she put her hand on my shoulder and said, "Thanks for helping me out of a jam!"

I smiled so wide one corner of

my mouth wasn't even in **America** anymore!

That's when my dad rushed up to me and I realized that I had forgotten I was probably in big trouble. "What happened to the box?" he asked me.

"I don't know!" I said. "It just disappeared!"

"It just disappeared?" he asked, with a *there is more to this story than you are telling me, Frannie* face.

"I don't know what happened!" I told him.

"Mr. Tilson went to look for it and he couldn't find it, either," my dad said.

"Let me wrap up here and we'll all go look for it, shall we?" Mrs. Zucker suggested.

When she was done, my dad and I went with her to look for the box. On our way, I saw Henry with her dad. She caught my eye and gave me a thumbs-up. That made all my **insides smile**. And my **mouth**, too. She was *Good Job, Frannie*-ing me!

It turns out the box wasn't even lost to begin with! It had just been pushed **farther** under the chair! It was there the whole time!

"Sometimes when people get **nervous**, they make very silly mistakes they would never make if they were calm," my dad explained. I guess I was so nervous about losing the box that my brain thought that I lost it when it was right there the whole time!

We dropped the juggling pins box with Ruby at the front desk so she could get in touch with the owner.

"Is there a conference about juggling

happening in the hotel?" I asked her. "Because that would be a conference I'd be very interested in going to."

"Not unless it's a supersecret conference," Ruby said.

That is when my mind started imagining how much fun a secret juggling conference would be. That is also when my father started talking to me about something that was **the opposite of fun**.

"Frannie, we've had a thousand conversations about responsibility," my dad said.

"But I helped Mrs. Zucker! I used my imagination, just like what the conference was all about!" I told him.

"Mrs. Zucker would not have needed help if you had been responsible and watched that box," he said.

"But I *was* being responsible!" I argued. "I had to make sure Henry wasn't quitting her job!"

"Whose responsibility is Henry's job?"

"Henry's," I answered, looking at the ground.

"And whose responsibility is your job?"

"Mine," I said, burning hot with humilification.

"Next time, what would you do differently?" my dad asked.

"I would worry about Henry not being at her job, and maybe tell a grown-up about it if they walked by, but I would just stay at my job because that is my responsibility."

"Very good. And just to be sure we never have this conversation again, when we get home I'm going to give you a new responsibility around the house. From now on, it's going to be your responsibility to keep an eye on the trash and take it out when it gets too full. Understood?"

I made sure my brain understood about my new responsibility.

"Understood," I told my father when I was absolutely sure.

And you will never believe what happened next.

An actual clown with a sad day look on his face walked by the information desk! Then, my father sent me a brain note. It said, "Don't even think about it for one second, Frances Bird Miller!" That is when I sent him a brain note that said, "I AM thinking about it for one second, but I will NOT follow that clown to see if there is a supersecret juggling conference. I do not want to take the garbage out every day of my entire worldwide life."

When my dad saw that I wasn't going to follow the clown, we stood side by side and watched him. He walked right through the lobby, past the table where Henry and I were sitting and through the revolving doors. He was probably going to get into his clown car with his other clown friends. That's when my dad took my hand and said, "C'mon, my little clown, let's go find your mother."

CHAPTER 12

The next morning, we took the Princessland shuttle bus with the Tilsons and some other people. The second I saw it up close, my eye sockets were shocktified.

There were the three **real, live castles** we saw on the drive to the hotel. Inside one of them was a tower room where they put a Rapunzel wig on you and you could let your hair hang out of the window. There were

boats in canals you could ride on,
and there was a zoo with real, live
elephants, which are my favorite
animal! They had real trains running
throughout the entire park. And you
could ride in them! There were real
princes, princesses, kings, and queens
in their gowns and crowns and capes.
They walked around and you could
meet them and **shake their hands**
and get your picture taken with them!
There was even royal money! It was
like **a giant's imagination** had
exploded all over the place.

That is when I wrote on my brain
paper to tell Mrs. Zucker that if
she wanted to understand about
imagination, THIS was the place to go.

We rode on carousels and bumper
cars and horse and carriages! Finally,

we saw the teacups and my mom gave a big gasp of excitement. She could not wait! I'd never seen my mom **so excited** for anything **so kiddish** before.

There was a long line for the teacups. When we finally got to the front, we saw the ride stopping to let people out. Everyone but one person got out. Do you know who it was?

Mrs. Zucker!

Finally it was our turn to ride the teacups. I sat with my mom and dad. Henry and Mr. Tilson sat in their own teacup. We held on to the middle handle. The ride started and we slowly **turned in our teacups** as we went around in a circle like on a carousel. I watched Mrs. Zucker throw her arms up and toss her head back. And when I looked at my mom, I was filled up to

the very top of my head with love and
happiness. Her eyes were closed and
her entire face was smiling: her mouth,
her cheeks, her eyebrows, her ears, and
even her hair! I love my mother *so, so,
so, so, so, so* much and I was so glad to be
with her while she was spinning around
and around in **a teacup of happiness**.

I went on the ride a machillion times (because that is my favorite number). I went in a teacup with my parents and Mrs. Zucker. Then I went in a teacup alone with my mom. Then I went alone with my dad. Then I went alone with Mrs. Zucker. Then I went alone with Henry, and then, finally, I went alone by myself. And by myself **again** and **again** and **again**.

I certainly loved being a guest speaker. And I certainly loved the idea of working at a hotel one day, but I was starting to wonder about **a career in teacups**. Of course, I would first have to find out if teacup ride workers had offices. If they did, I would move to Florida and work here. We could all live in the castle with Rapunzel! Or even the palace with the kings and queens.

Then every year when Mrs. Zucker would come to give her speech, we'd say, "Come stay with us in the castle, Mrs. Zucker!"

And every day, my mom, dad, Mrs. Zucker, and I could ride the teacups and laugh and laugh and say, "Is it just my imagination or are we having the best time ever?"

I certainly do have a big imagination. But looking at my mom and dad and all our new friends, I realized that my real life is just as big.

THE END.